YOU CRACK THE CASE

RUSSIAN GOLD

STEVE BARLOW & STEVE SKIDMORE
ILLUSTRATED BY DAVID COUSENS

LONDON·SYDNEY

First published in 2011
by Franklin Watts

Text © Steve Barlow and Steve Skidmore 2011
Illustrations by David Cousens © Franklin Watts 2011
"The 2 Steves" logo used with kind permission of Orchard Books
Cover design by Peter Scoulding

Franklin Watts
338 Euston Road
London NW1 3BH

Franklin Watts Australia
Level 17/207 Kent Street
Sydney, NSW 2000

A CIP catalogue record for this book
is available from the British Library.

ISBN: 978 0 7496 9285 8

1 3 5 7 9 10 8 6 4 2

An adventure where YOU
crack the case!

This book is not like others you may have read. In this story YOU have to make decisions to solve the crime. Each section of this book is numbered. At the end of each section, YOU will have to make a choice. The choice YOU make will lead to a different section of the book.

Some choices will be correct, others will not. You must make the right choices by looking at the evidence, solving puzzles or even breaking codes. Make sure that you LOOK carefully at the pictures – they *could* give you vital clues.

If you make a bad decision you may receive a warning from your boss, or get thrown off the case. Some of your decisions could even be fatal!

Record how many BAD DECISIONS and WARNINGS you get from your boss. When you have cracked the case – or been kicked off it – you'll get a Crime Team Agent Rating that will show how well – or how badly – you've done.

You are the leader of Crime Team, a section of the International Police Federation based in New York City, USA. You are one of the world's leading experts in cracking cases that no one else can. You have solved crimes across the globe and have made many enemies, who would like to see you dead…

YOUR MISSION

» To aid and support national police forces anywhere in the world.
» To tackle the toughest cases and solve mysteries that others cannot.

YOUR TEAM

Your team contains the best of the best – top investigative experts from around the world. You will have to make decisions about how to use your team and whose skills will be best suited to help solve the crime.

YOUR BOSS
COMMANDER TUCKER

Ex-military, ex-New York Police Department, ex-CIA and currently your bad-ass boss. Given half a chance, Commander Tucker will chew your butt. He will alert you to BAD DECISIONS and give you WARNINGS. He might even THROW YOU OFF the case!

YOUR SIDEKICK
LEON PEREZ

JOB: Your constant sidekick and legman – Leon does all the stuff you're too busy to do yourself and is also the "muscle".

EXPERTISE: A ballistics expert with a wide knowledge of all types of weapon.

NOTES: It is said he can smell a bullet and tell you which gun it came from – he's that good!

DOCTOR ANUSHA DAS

JOB: Forensic pathologist
EXPERTISE: Brilliant at establishing the time
and cause of death of a victim.
NOTES: Extensive knowledge of poisons
and diseases.

SUN LIN

JOB: Forensic scientist
EXPERTISE: An expert at fingerprinting, DNA
analysis and other forensic techniques.
NOTES: Has the ability to remember everything
she has seen or heard. Never forgets a face,
remembers every crime report and excellent
at finding all kinds of information.

DARIUS KING ("BUGS")

JOB: Computer expert
EXPERTISE: A genius at hacking, data retrieval and electronic surveillance.
NOTES: Is an expert in using computers to help with HID (Human Identification at a Distance) to identify suspects and criminals.

TODD BLACKWOOD

JOB: Profiler (forensic psychologist)
EXPERTISE: Can "get inside" the minds of criminals and predict what they will do next.
NOTES: Also an expert in espionage, counter-espionage and terrorism.

» NOW GO TO SECTION 1.

1

You and the rest of Crime Team are in Moscow, Russia. You have been told that you are to work on a joint operation with the Russian Security Services and the CIA.

You and the team are sitting in the lobby of the Hotel National, overlooking the Kremlin and Red Square. You have been waiting over an hour for your contact to turn up. The team are not happy!

"Why do we have to be here?" moans Perez. "I thought that we were supposed to solve crimes and as far as I can see, there isn't a crime to solve!"

"Don't wish for things, Leon," says Sun Lin. "They just might happen!"

"Tucker said this would be good training for us," you explain. "But I still don't know why we're here – he didn't tell me."

At that moment, a man and a woman head towards you. The woman smiles and offers her hand. "I'm Jenni James, your CIA contact."

"And who's your friend?" you ask, shaking her hand firmly.

"This is Viktor Pavlov, Deputy Head of the Russian Security Service," Jenni says.

"And what brings the Russian and American secret services together?" you say.

"I will tell you, but we need to go somewhere

a little more private," says the man. "You should come with us now."

» **If you want to leave with them, go to 9.**
» **If you wish to check their ID first, go to 17.**

2

"I can't see how they got in during the ambush," you say. "They must have been inside the truck when we left the airport. I think we take that as our starting point."

"That makes no sense," says Anusha. "We saw the gold being loaded – there was no one in the back of the truck when we left."

Perez agrees. "And to cut a hole in the floor of the truck means that they must have had some cutting gear already inside. That wasn't there either. They must have got in during the ambush."

You realise that you are wrong and Anusha and Perez are right…

» **YOU'VE MADE A BAD DECISION!**
Make a note of it and go to 28.

3

You tell the team to meet in the lobby before six and then head up to your hotel room to talk to Tucker.

You switch the phone to secure mode and call him. You tell him about the threat of robbery.

"That's why I sent you to Moscow," he explains. "I couldn't tell you while someone might have listened in, but we've heard that there is a mole – an insider – involved in the shipment of the gold who is giving information to the Russian mafia. I need you to keep an eye on the situation and report back if you suspect anyone. We need to catch the informer. Trust no one and stay with the gold at all times."

You ring off and wonder who the informer might be.

» Go to 34.

4

You think about the laser cutter. "Why does the machine have that code written on it?" you wonder.

"It's just the serial number," says Anusha.

"But there are no numbers in it and it's not written in the Russian alphabet. If it was from the Russian military, surely the code would be written in the Cyrillic alphabet, like Pavlov's ID card."

You look at it again.

image enhancement...

"There are a lot of Ys in it," says Anusha.
You think where you have heard something like
that before…

Leon shakes his head. "There's also a Y in 'Why
are we wasting our time?' Let's get the dogs onto
Pavlov!"

» **If you want to discuss the code, go to 33.**
» **If you want to accuse Pavlov, go to 38.**

5

"Leon's right!" you snap. "This is not a Crime
Team case."

Pavlov turns to Jenni. "I never wanted these
people on this mission. This fool's attitude proves
I was right!"

You jump up. "Say that again," you threaten.

Jenni James holds up a hand. "OK, children,
time out." She reaches into her bag for her phone,
but as she pulls it out a file drops to the floor.

You bend down to help her, but she waves you
away and jabs at the phone's touchpad.

"Tell Tucker to call me." She rings off. "Viktor,
sit down, please. We need these people." She turns
to you. "And you need to stop being such an—"
She is cut off by the sound of Yankee Doodle
Dandy playing.

"Nice ringtone," says Perez. "Very American.

Very patriotic."

She hands the phone to you. The next two minutes are filled with the sound of Tucker shouting at you. He calms down a little and tells you to call him when you get back to the hotel. He ends with a warning. "Be nice to the Russians or I'll have your sorry butt out of the Crime Team!"

» **YOU'VE BEEN GIVEN A WARNING!**
  Make a note of it and go to 25.

6

You call Pavlov and Jenni James over and show them the massive hole cut into the bottom of the empty truck.

Pavlov looks stunned. "How can this be?"

"That's what we need to find out, Viktor," you say. "Good job we're here to help get you out of your mess."

"What do we do now, boss?" asks Anusha.

You think for a moment. "We need to check out forensics on the truck and also get back to where we were attacked."

» **If you wish to split the team up, go to 18.**

» **To keep the team together, go to 35.**

7

You tell Pavlov about your conversation with Tucker, and warn him there might be an informer.

He is furious! "How dare you insult the Russian Security Forces with these lies! I will not have such people working with me!"

Despite your protests, he orders you and the team out of the airport. Jenni James is furious. "You were supposed to work with him!"

» **YOU'VE BEEN THROWN OFF
   THE CASE!**

   To see how you rate as a detective, go to 46.

8

"I'll call Pavlov," you say.

Todd cuts in. "Hang on, boss. You said yourself, 'Don't trust anyone.' The insider could be Pavlov or one of his people. We need to review the evidence and see if we can find the answer ourselves before we try to get the gold back."

The others agree – Todd is right.

» **YOU'VE MADE A BAD DECISION!**
   Make a note of it and go to 43.

9

"OK. Come on team," you say.

The man is not impressed. "That is not very good security," he says. "Just leaving with, how do you say? Any old Tom, Dick and Harry…"

You groan. You should have asked for their ID.

The man turns to the woman. "Perhaps I should tell Commander Tucker to employ more professional people?"

"I'm sure it was just a mistake," says the woman. "Naturally, the Crime Team would trust a member of the CIA." She turns back to you. "Do you want to see our ID?"

» **YOU'VE MADE A MISTAKE, *BUT GOT***
   AWAY WITH IT!
   Go to 17.

"OK, I just hope you're right," you say.

By now the attackers are being forced back as the Russian troops continue to fight back. You make your way to the SUV and check that the rest of the team members are OK. Thankfully, they are.

"Time to keep our heads down and let the troops sort it out," you tell them.

After another fifteen minutes of fierce fighting, all but one of the attackers is dead. The remaining man tries to drive away in the attack car, but a volley of bullets shreds the tyres. The car spins out of control, hits a building and explodes. Quiet descends on the street.

"What do we do now, boss?" asks Anusha. "Get out of here or try to find out who those guys were?"

» **If you want to search the area for clues now, go to 41.**

» **If you want to get the gold to the secure vault, go to 24.**

11

"The insider is you, Pavlov," you say. "You're working with the mafia!"

Pavlov bursts out laughing. "You are even more stupid than I thought! Where is your evidence?"

"You knew the route the convoy was taking. The armoured truck stopped just at the right spot, over the sewer entrance. And we found a laser cutter in the sewer – only the military could get hold of that."

Pavlov shakes his head. "Miss James also knew the route." Jenni James nods her head.

"And there are many soldiers in the military who could be bribed by the mafia to get hold of a laser cutter. Get out of my office before I have you arrested. I have to talk to your boss."

You step outside.

After ten minutes, your phone rings. It is Tucker. "You fool! How dare you accuse a top Russian agent of treason and robbery without solid evidence? You may have located the gold, but we still don't know who the insider is. I'm gonna get someone else to investigate. You're off the case, dumbo!"

» **YOU'VE BEEN THROWN OFF THE CASE!**
To see how you rate as a detective, go to 46.

12

"Hold your horses, Leon," you say. "Let's find out some more facts."

At that moment the sound of Yankee Doodle Dandy cuts through the air. Jenni James smiles. "My phone's ringtone," she says.

"Nice tune," says Bugs. "Very American. Very patriotic."

As she takes the phone out from her bag, a file drops out.

You bend down to help her, but she waves you away and answers the call. "It's Tucker," she says and hands you the phone.

You listen for a couple of minutes as Tucker tells you in no uncertain terms that you have got to be nice to the Russians.

"I was being," you protest.

"Make sure you carry on that way," he warns you. "And I need to speak to you when you are back in the hotel." He rings off.

» **Go to 25.**

13

You dive out of the car, firing at the attackers and sprint to the armoured truck that Todd and Perez were travelling in. Although the engine is still running, the truck is on fire.

You head to the cab and wrench at the door, but can't open it. The driver is slumped against the window. Bullets whistle through the air as the fight continues.

At that moment, Pavlov appears with a fire extinguisher. He quickly puts out the fire. You lean in through the shattered windscreen and reach for the driver's door release. You pull the door open and bundle the driver out – he is dead. Pavlov presses a button to unlock the rear doors.

"See if your colleagues are all right." Pavlov hurries back towards his troops, who are fighting hard.

You dash to the back of the armoured truck as Todd and Perez stumble out.

"You two OK?" you ask.

They nod, dazed.

» **If you want to get the gold out of there, go to 39.**

» **If you want to fight the attackers, go to 19.**

You recall Tucker's words: "Trust no one".

"We'll keep this to ourselves," you tell the others.

You ring Pavlov. "We've drawn a blank. We're going to head back to the hotel. If you need our help, call us."

"Giving up so soon? I thought Crime Team were supposed to be the best..." He rings off.

An hour later you are sitting with the team in a hotel conference room. Bugs has the information you asked for.

"There are many entrances to the sewers, but I also hacked into the Moscow surveillance camera system and checked on all movement around the various entrances. I got lucky! This came up."

Bugs shows you a video of a van.

"I've followed the van on the Moscow traffic camera network. It's heading northwest out of the city. It seems to making for St Petersburg – that's about 300 miles away, so if that's where they're headed they should be there in about six hours. I've programmed one of our surveillance satellites to keep tracking it."

"Well done, Bugs. So, we know where the gold is. But who is behind the robbery? Who is the insider?"

Perez shrugs. "Simple. Why don't we get the Russians to stop the van and question the driver?"

» To review the evidence, go to 43.

» To follow Leon's suggestion, go to 8.

15

As you are walking through the lobby, your phone rings. It is Tucker.

"I thought I told you to call me when you got to the hotel!" he says.

You curse – you should have remembered! "I've only just arrived at the hotel. I'm in the lobby," you reply.

"OK," he grunts. "Get yourself to somewhere you can't be heard and call me back. I've got some important information." He rings off.

You breathe a sigh of relief. Tucker didn't give you a warning!

» **YOU MADE A MISTAKE, *BUT GOT AWAY WITH IT!***
Go to 3.

16

You ring Pavlov and tell him you want to meet.

"Meet me at my office in an hour. On your own," he adds.

You tell the others what he has said.

"It's a setup, boss," says Perez.

"Maybe, maybe not," you reply. "We'll know soon enough."

An hour later you enter Pavlov's office. He is waiting for you. Jenni James is also there.

"What is this all about?" asks Pavlov. "Do you have any information about the gold?"

"Yes," you nod. "I know where it is. Bugs is tracking it as I speak."

Pavlov and Jenni both looked shocked. "Tell me where it is!" demands Pavlov.

"In a minute. I also want to tell you who organised the robbery. I want to tell you who the insider is."

» **If you think it is Pavlov, go to 11.**
» **If you think it is someone else, go to 26.**

17

"OK. Show me your ID," you say.

The woman shows you her CIA card. Then the man shows you his identification.

командир
Виктор Павлов

Заместитель руководителя
Федеральной службы
безопасности Русской
Федерации

РОССИЯ
ФСБ

ФСБ РФ

» **If you wish to ask about Pavlov's ID, go to 44.**

» **If you wish to find out where you are going, go to 32.**

18

"OK, we'll split up to cover more ground," you tell the team. "We'll meet up later. Bugs, Sun Lin, you check out forensics on this armoured truck. Anusha, Todd and Perez, come with me and we'll head back to the scene of the attack."

Pavlov speaks up. "I will have to stay here – I need to contact the government ministers."

"I'll stay here with you Viktor, and report back to my people," says Jenni James. She turns to you. "Keep me posted – you have my number."

You leave Bugs and Sun Lin, jump in an SUV and head back across the city.

By the time you arrive, the Russian troops that Pavlov ordered to stay behind have sealed off the area. You show your ID and look around the scene of the ambush.

"How could the attackers have got into the armoured truck?" wonders Perez. "And then got the gold out?"

"Only two solutions," you say. "They got in during the ambush or they were already inside…"

"So what do you think?" asks Anusha.

» **If you think the attackers were already inside the armoured truck, go to 2.**

» **If you think they got inside during the ambush, go to 28.**

19

You take out your gun and begin shooting.
You hit one of the attackers and he drops to the
ground. However, there are too many of them.

Another of the attacking men sees you and
aims his machine gun at you. You are an easy
target, and there is nothing you can do as the
bullets tear through your body. You slump to the
ground, with Sun Lin's screams ringing in your
ears.

» **YOU HAVE PAID THE ULTIMATE
PRICE.**
Start the case again by going to 1.

20

You think about the number plate of the
attacker's car.

"I'm sure we've seen a number plate like that
before," you tell the team.

"Let's not waste any more time," says Perez. "Let's just get Pavlov behind bars."

» **If you want to review more evidence, go to 4.**

» **If you agree with Perez, go to 38.**

21

Pavlov calls up a Mil Mi-14 military helicopter. Soon you and the Crime Team are in the air, heading for St Petersburg airport.

Bugs looks up from his laptop computer. "Our spy satellite lost the suspect van in St Petersburg – too much traffic."

"Doesn't matter," you say. "We know where they're headed."

You arrive at the airport. Pavlov's men order the airport authorities to hold all outgoing flights. You wait for the van containing the gold to arrive.

Two hours later, it has still not shown up. Pavlov is furious. "You've made me shut down one of Russia's busiest airports for no reason," he storms, "and on top of that, you've lost the gold! When I tell your Commander Tucker about this, you will be finished!"

You know Pavlov is right. As soon as Tucker hears about your failure, he tells you to get back home ASAP!

» **YOU'VE BEEN THROWN OFF THE CASE!**
To see how you rate as a detective, go to 46.

22

You ring Pavlov and tell him your news.

"I will see you at the hotel," he says and rings off.

Half an hour later, you meet up with Pavlov and Jenni James at the hotel. Pavlov is grim faced. "Thank you for your help, but we don't need you anymore, you are to go home. We will deal with this."

You are amazed! "You are kidding me? Tell him, Jenni…"

Jenni James shakes her head. "Orders from the top. You're all heading back to New York pronto!"

You protest, but it is no good.

On the way to the airport you take a call from Tucker. He is furious. "I told you to trust no one! You shouldn't have told anyone what you found! We've lost a truckload of gold and we don't know who the insider was! We're gonna have serious words when you get back!"

» **YOU'VE BEEN THROWN OFF THE CASE!**
To see how you rate as a detective, go to 46.

23

"We need Crime Team with the gold, Pavlov," you insist. "Otherwise we aren't going anywhere."

Pavlov scowls. "Very well. You can put two of your team into the first armoured truck. The second armoured truck is already full with gold. That is my final offer to you."

You realise that there is no point arguing further. You nod OK. "Perez and Todd, you can go in with the gold. Bugs, Sun Lin and Anusha, you travel with me in the SUV."

The convoy sets off and is soon travelling at speed through the Moscow streets.

Suddenly, a car cuts out from a side road and overtakes your SUV. A man leans out of the window holding a grenade launcher. There is a whoosh and a dart of flame. The armoured truck with Perez and Todd inside is hit. It bursts into flames!

The whole convoy comes to a screeching halt. Several hooded men jump out of the attacking car and begin firing. The Russian troops pour out of the trucks and return fire. It is chaos!

» **To try to help Perez and Todd, go to 13.**
» **If you want to return fire, go to 19.**
» **To tell the driver to drive away quickly, go to 36.**

24

As you head towards the armoured trucks, Pavlov and Jenni James appear.

"Get your team to secure the area – you should come with us and the gold," you say.

"I give the orders," says Pavlov.

"But they are bad ones, Pavlov," you snap. "You nearly lost the gold. No one was supposed to know the convoy route."

"Handbags away," says Jenni. "Viktor, let's get the gold to the bank. Then we can sort out who is behind this mess."

Pavlov scowls and grunts agreement. He rounds up a squad of men to stay behind and secure the area. The other troops jump back into the remaining trucks. A new driver is found for the damaged armoured truck and soon the convoy moves off once again. You follow behind in the SUV.

You finally reach the bank and pull up in a courtyard.

You jump out of the SUV. "Perez, Sun Lin, help open up the second gold truck. I'll sort out the damaged one."

They nod and head off.

You open up the damaged armoured truck and check that the gold is intact. You breathe a sigh of relief – it is all there.

A minute later, you hear Perez calling out for you. You hurry over to him.

Sun Lin is shaking her head and pointing into the back of the other armoured truck. There's a hole inside where the gold should be! "Looks like Leon got his crime to solve. The gold has gone!"

» Go to 6.

25

You hand back the phone. "OK, tell me more about the operation," you say.

"The gold is being taken from the airport in armoured vehicles this evening," replies Jenni James. "The US government wanted you to make sure the handover goes smoothly."

"Why can't the CIA deal with it?" asks Anusha.

Jenni James stares at Viktor. "The Russians want 'unofficial' observers. That's why you're here."

Pavlov cuts in. "Miss James and I have worked out the plan for the movement of the gold. We will have several armoured vehicles and over 30 troops guarding the gold…"

"What route will you be taking?" you ask.

"Only Miss James and I know that," replies the Russian. "We will give this information to the drivers, when we have picked up the gold. The fewer people that know the route, the less chance there is of a robbery."

"Is there a chance of a robbery from organised gangs?" you ask.

Jenni James looks at Viktor. He shakes his head. "No."

» If you think they are holding something back, go to 29.

» If you wish to return to the hotel, go to 37.

26

You take out your phone and tap at the numbers.

"What on earth are you doing?" says Jenni.

The sound of Yankee Doodle Dandy fills the room.

"Your ringtone I believe, Miss James."

"What does this mean?" asks Pavlov.

"It means that Jenni James is the insider; the mole. She is the one working with the Russian mafia and she helped organise the robbery."

"How do you know?" asks Pavlov.

"Her phone number was written in code on the laser cutter we found in the sewer."

"The idiot who supplied my guys with the laser cutter must have had a lousy memory. Looks like you got my number," says Jenni James.

"She also knew the route and could make sure that the attack happened at exactly the right place. There's more. It was a car with American diplomatic plates that was used in the attack. She also didn't want me to move the gold during the attack as she knew the team in the sewer needed time to cut into the truck and unload the gold."

"Am I right, Miss James?"

Jenni James smiles and holds out her hands. "So, you got me."

Pavlov is puzzled. "But why?"

"Viktor, that sort of gold can buy a girl a lot of shoes…"

You interrupt. "Never mind the smart remarks. Where are your men taking the gold?"

She grins. "Guess you'll have to think deeply about that one."

Pavlov signals his men to take Jenni James out. Then he turns to you. "All right, we have our informer. But where is the gold going?"

"Bugs thought St Petersburg," you tell him. "Do you have a map?"

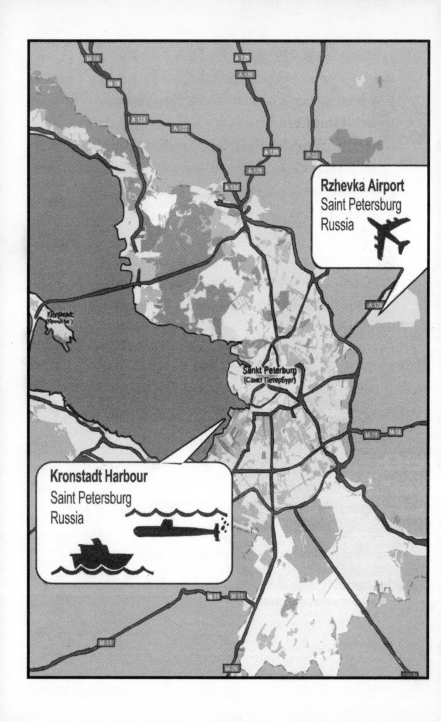

Rzhevka Airport
Saint Petersburg
Russia

Kronstadt Harbour
Saint Petersburg
Russia

It takes a few seconds for Pavlov to pull a map up on his computer screen.

"Think deeply about where the gold is," you muse. "Hmmmm."

» **If you think the gold is heading for the airport, go to 21.**

» **If you think the gold is heading for the harbour, go to 40.**

27

"OK, if you say so, Viktor."

"Can I have a word with you?" Jenni James takes you out of the Russian agent's earshot. "You were right in the first place," she says. "I think it is a good idea that Crime Team members are in the vehicles."

"I don't want to upset Pavlov."

"Stand up for yourself," she whispers.

You remember Tucker's words. "Stay with the gold". You realise that she is right.

» **YOU MADE A BAD DECISION!**
Make a note of it and go to 23.

28

"OK," you say. "We saw no one getting in the armoured truck at the airport. How did they get into the truck during the ambush?"

"The attack lasted nearly half an hour," says Perez. "But I didn't see any of the attackers get near the armoured truck."

"Maybe one of the Russian guards got inside

during the fight," suggests Todd.

You look around. "I think there's more to it than that," you say.

» **Go to 31.**

29

"OK, if there's no threat why have you got a Top Secret file on the Russian mafia?" you ask.

Jenni James looks a little embarrassed. She stares at Pavlov, who nods.

"All right," she says. "We've received reports of a clear and present threat to the gold."

"If you mean a robbery, why don't you say a robbery?" says Perez.

"Where are these threats coming from?" you ask.

She hands you a sheet from the file. "The Moscow Bratva. They are one of the most dangerous organised gangs in the world. They have over five thousand members and deal in every kind of illegal activity you can think of and then more besides."

Viktor shakes his head. "They will not try anything. We have a large armed escort and the route is secret. Do not worry about the mafia."

"We'll leave for the airport at six tonight," says Jenni James. "Until then, please return to the hotel... Here's my phone number, if you need to call me."

CENTRAL INTELLIGENCE AGENCY

JENNI JAMES
MOBILE:06066661236

1 8 7 2 5 1 1 1 0

You look at her number. "That's a lot of sixes."

"My favourite number." Jenni smiles. "Catch you at six."

You and the team return to the hotel. Perez is still moaning. "I still don't understand why we have to be here…"

"Like they said, to make sure it goes smoothly," you say. "And if it doesn't, then you'll have your crime to solve."

» **If you wish to speak to Tucker, go to 3.**
» **If you want to get some rest before the operation, go to 15.**

30

"We're getting out of here. Perez, Todd, get over to the SUV and tell Bugs to follow me." They nod and run off.

Ignoring Jenni's protests, you climb into the cab of the armoured truck and pull away. Luckily the damage to the truck is not too severe.

Bugs is soon behind you driving the SUV. You hurtle down the street. However, you only get a couple of hundred metres before you see a pick-up truck blocking the road. Several masked men stand waiting for you. Jenni was right! You've fallen into a trap! You push the accelerator to the floor.

Ahead of you there is a flash of light. A rocket grenade is heading your way! You try to veer left, but are too late. The grenade hits. The last thing you feel is a searing heat as the cab is engulfed in a fireball.

» **YOUR FAILURE HAS COST YOU YOUR LIFE.**

If you wish to start the case again, go to 1.

31

You point at the sewer cover. "Isn't that where the armoured truck stopped?"

You sprint over to the cover. "Help me with this, Perez."

The two of you lift up the cover and peer into the gloom. "I'll take a look." You head down the ladder. At the bottom there is a strange looking machine. You take a picture of it with your smartphone. "Gotcha," you say. "A laser cutter. That's how they got into the truck…"

Leon, Todd and Anusha follow you down to explore the sewer. However, there is no sign of any gold, so you head back to the surface. "We need to know where this sewer leads," you say.

Your phone rings; it is Bugs. "The hole was cut with a laser," he says.

"Yeah, we've just found it," you reply. You send Bugs the picture of the machine via your smartphone.

"That is a serious piece of kit," he says. "Only the military and secret services could have access to that sort of thing."

"OK, Bugs, I need you to find out details about where this sewer goes. Meet us back at the hotel with the info."

» **If you want to tell Pavlov about your discovery, go to 22.**
» **If you want to keep it to yourself, go to 14.**

32

"Where are we going?" you ask.

"To our HQ," replies Viktor. "We will brief you there."

You head outside to a waiting people carrier. Soon you and the team are travelling through the busy Moscow streets. You arrive at the HQ and are shown into a briefing room.

"So why are we here?" you ask.

Jenni James answers. "The US government has reached an agreement with the Russians to supply the US with oil and gas supplies for the next twenty years. They are paying for it with gold bars – millions of dollars' worth. The gold is arriving at a military airport tonight. It is then being taken to a secure bank vault. You have been asked to oversee the transfer and make sure that nothing goes wrong."

Perez stands up. "We're not security guards! We're the Crime Team. This isn't for us!"

» **If you agree with Perez, go to 5.**
» **If you want to hear more about the operation, go to 12.**

33

"There are a lot of sixes in this number," you say.

Perez yawns. "What are you going on about?"

You take out your smartphone. "I've just got an idea…"

"PY PYYYY Q W E Y," you say to yourself...
"I think we need to meet up with Pavlov and
Jenni James."

"I think we need to let Tucker know that
Pavlov is the insider," replies Perez.

» **If you want a meeting with Pavlov and
James, go to 16.**
» **If you want to call Tucker and accuse
Pavlov, go to 38.**

34

Just before six, you meet the team in the lobby.

"Have you all got your guns?" you ask.
The team nods. "Let's hope we
don't need them."

Jenni James arrives
and takes you outside
to an SUV.

"It's an American embassy vehicle," she explains. "It has special number plates. 004 for America. D for diplomat. It'll help get us through at the military airport."

You travel through the Moscow streets and finally arrive at the military airport. You and the team are taken to a high-security compound. There are many armed soldiers guarding the gold as it is loaded into two armoured security trucks.

Pavlov is overseeing operations. He nods at you.

"Any more information on the mafia?" you ask.

He shakes his head. "No, I don't think there is anything to worry about."

» **If you want to tell him about the insider, go to 7.**

» **If you wish to keep this information to yourself, go to 42.**

35

"We'll stick together and look at the truck first."

Perez shakes his head. "Boss, don't you think that we should split up – we'll save time. We don't want to miss any clues by staying together. We can then meet up and report back everything we've found."

The rest of the team nod agreement. You realise that Perez is correct. You're glad that Tucker isn't here to bawl you out for making a mistake!

» **YOU'VE MADE A BAD DECISION *BUT GOT AWAY WITH IT!***

Go to 18.

36

"Get us out of here!" you shout at the driver.

Anusha reaches for the door handle. "What about Todd and Leon?"

"Stay in the car!" you answer. "It's safer in here – Todd and Leon will have to look after themselves!"

"What sort of leader are you?" shouts Sun Lin.

Before you can answer there is a huge explosion as a rocket grenade hits the SUV. You try to get out, but you are too late as the vehicle explodes in a fireball of noise and heat.

» **YOUR COWARDICE HAS COST YOU YOUR LIFE.**

Begin the case again by going to 1.

37

"Let's get back to the hotel," you say.

"Not yet," Todd whispers. "They're not telling us everything." He nods at the file that Jenni James dropped. "If there's nothing wrong, then why have they got a Top Secret file on the Russian mafia?"

You realise that Todd is right. You decide to ask Jenni about the file, but you should have spotted that yourself!

» **YOU MADE A BAD DECISION!**
   Make a note of it and go to 29.

38

You ring Tucker. "The insider is Viktor Pavlov."

"And what's your evidence?" he asks.

"He knew the route and the laser cutting equipment was military."

"What else?"

"Nothing."

Tucker explodes! "What sort of fool do you think I am? I can't go to the Russian government and say that one of their most important agents is working with the mafia without any real evidence. There would be hell to pay! Get back here now, you're all off the case!"

» **YOU'VE BEEN THROWN OFF THE CASE!**
  To see how you rate as a detective, go to 46.

39

"We need to get some of the gold away from here," you tell the others. You look over the damaged armoured truck.

"We can still drive this away…"

At that moment, you see Jenni James running towards you. You explain what you want to do.

She shakes her head. "Don't drive away yet. Keep the armoured trucks together. I think this might be a trick to separate the gold from the troops."

» **If you want to ignore her advice, go to 30.**
» **If you want to take her advice, go to 10.**

40

"They've reached St Petersburg – our spy satellite has lost them in traffic."

"All right, Bugs." You turn to Pavlov. "Are your men deployed at the port?"

He nods. "This had better not be a wild-goose chase."

You land on a helipad at the port. Pavlov leads you to the lighthouse overlooking the docks. "We should get a good view from here," he says. "If your guess is correct."

From the balcony of the lighthouse, you scan the harbour with binoculars. Pavlov lets out an exclamation. "There's a submarine in port. I wasn't expecting that."

"I was," you tell him. He stares at you.

There is no further time for talk. The van carrying the gold has arrived. You watch as Pavlov's men pour out of their hiding places and surround the vehicle.

The gang surrender without a fight.

Moments later and without its haul of gold, you see the submarine cast off its mooring lines and head out to sea before the Russian forces can board it.

» **Go to 45.**

41

"Let's find out who those attackers were," you tell the team.

"Shouldn't we be getting the gold out of here?" says Bugs.

"I want to find out who is responsible for—"

At that moment your phone rings. You answer. It is Tucker. "What the heck is going on over there?" he asks. "We've had intelligence from our spy satellites that there's been some sort of attack."

You tell Tucker what has happened. "We're going to try to search the area for clues."

"Leave that to the Russians!" shouts Tucker. "You just make sure the gold is delivered. Do your job or I'll get someone else to do it!"

He rings off. You look at the team. "OK, we'll get the gold out of here."

Perez sniggers.

» YOU MADE A BAD DECISION!
Make a note of it and go to 24.

42

"Trust nobody." You remember what Tucker said and decide not to tell Pavlov about the insider. "So what's the plan? What's the route?"

Jenni James shakes her head. "That has to remain secret. You can see this though. This is how

the convoy will be made up. The gold will be in
the two armoured trucks."

She hands you a diagram.

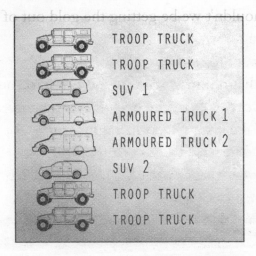

	TROOP TRUCK
	TROOP TRUCK
	SUV 1
	ARMOURED TRUCK 1
	ARMOURED TRUCK 2
	SUV 2
	TROOP TRUCK
	TROOP TRUCK

"I will be in the lead SUV," says Pavlov.
"I'll join you, Viktor," says Jenni James. "I don't
want you to feel lonely!" You wonder if she
knows about the insider and that is why she wants
to stay close to Pavlov. She turns to you. "You and
the team can travel in the SUV behind the trucks
carrying the gold."

You recall what Tucker said about staying with
the gold. "I think we should put my team in the
armoured trucks with the gold."

Jenni looks at Pavlov. He shakes his head.

» **If you want to insist, go to 23.**
» **If you accept Pavlov's decision, go to 27.**

43

"So what have we got so far?" you ask.

The team discuss the evidence. You write it down.

- Known threat to gold
- Jenni James had Russian mafia secret file
- Mafia behind it on their own?
- Tucker warns about insider
- Number plate of attacking car – 004 D 36316
- Gold stolen whilst attack took place
- Truck had to be stopped at exact spot
- Route – arranged by Pavlov
- Laser cutter – military equipment
- Code number P Y P Y Y Y Y Q W E Y

"It looks pretty clear to me who the insider is," says Perez. "It's gotta be Pavlov."

"Maybe," you say. "But are we missing something?"

» If you want to talk more about the evidence, go to 20.

» If you think Pavlov is the insider, go to 38.

44

"It's your picture, but what do the words say?" you ask.

"It tells you who I am," replies Viktor, sarcastically. "It is Russian."

"It's a type of Cyrillic alphabet," says Sun Lin. "Very different from our alphabet."

You smile. "How do I know it doesn't say 'criminal boss'?"

"It's OK, boss," says Sun Lin. "It says that Pavlov is who he says he is!"

Viktor scowls. Jenni laughs. "You speak Russian like me, Miss Lin."

Sun Lin nods. "I speak many languages, Miss James."

Pavlov turns to you. "Perhaps you too should learn Russian, then you would be able to know that people are who they say they are."

"People aren't always who they say they are," you reply. "And I don't have the time at the moment. OK, you are Viktor Pavlov, now let's get going…"

» Go to 32.

45

An hour later, Pavlov has finished the mopping-up operation and invites you and your team to his temporary headquarters.

"I have a good deal to thank you for," he says. "If the attackers had succeeded in getting the gold aboard that submarine, they could have taken it anywhere in the world." He gives you a hard stare. "How did you know their plans?"

"Jenni James," you say. "When I asked her where the gold was, she told me to think deeply about the answer. As soon as I saw the submarine icon on the map, I knew what she meant. That's the problem with the CIA – some of them think they're so much smarter than anyone else, they can't help showing off."

"Mr Tucker says that he is very happy with you," says Pavlov. He turns to Leon. "Mr Perez, I heard that you thought I was the insider."

"Never crossed my mind," replies Perez.

Pavlov cracks a smile for the first time since you met him. "At any rate, you found the mole and saved the gold. But the Russian mafia are very powerful. Some day soon, no doubt they will strike again. I am sure that we are going to be working on more operations together…"

You smile. "Well, Viktor. It looks like the beginning of a beautiful friendship!"

» **You've cracked the case – well done!**
   Go to 46 to see how you rate as a detective.

46

How do you rate as a
Crime Team detective?

WASHOUT – if you were THROWN OFF THE CASE.
Polish up your detective skills and go back to 1.

AMATEUR – if you received a WARNING.
You need to try harder. See if you can do better on
other CRIME TEAM cases.

⭐ **ONE-STAR AGENT –** no warnings, but made THREE
or more BAD DECISIONS.
You need to boost your detecting skills. See if you can
stay more alert on other CRIME TEAM cases.

⭐ ⭐ **TWO-STAR AGENT –** no warnings, but made TWO
BAD DECISIONS.
Maybe you're lacking in confidence. Try looking for less
help on other CRIME TEAM cases.

⭐ ⭐ ⭐ **THREE-STAR AGENT –** no warnings, but made
ONE BAD DECISION.
You're a worthy leader of CRIME TEAM – well done!
But can you do as well on other CRIME TEAM cases?

⭐ **FIRST-CLASS CRIME TEAM AGENT –** no warnings,
and made no bad decisions.
You're a genius detective! Bet you can't do as well on
other CRIME TEAM cases…

Want to read more "You Are The Hero" adventures? Well, why not try these...

Also by the 2Steves: iHorror

Fight your fear. Choose your fate.

978 1 40830 985 8 pb
978 1 40831 476 0 eBook

978 1 40830 986 5 pb
978 1 40831 477 7 eBook

978 1 40830 988 9 pb
978 1 40831 479 1 eBook

978 1 40830 987 2 pb
978 1 40831 478 4 eBook

BATTLE BOOKS

by Gary Smailes

Take up your weapons and prepare to fight your own battle...

978 1 4451 0112 5 pb
978 1 4451 0839 1 eBook

978 1 4451 0113 2 pb
978 1 4451 0840 7 eBook

978 1 4451 0114 9 pb
978 14451 0841 4 eBook

978 1 4451 0115 6 pb
978 1 4451 0842 1 eBook